Paddington

Minds the House

MICHAEL BOND

Paddington

Minds the House

illustrated by R.W. ALLEY

HarperCollins *Children's Books*

One morning, Mrs Brown and Mrs Bird went out for the day and left Paddington to look after the house.

"I shall wash up all the breakfast things while you are gone," he said. "And then, if I have any time left over I may do some 'Spring Cleaning'."

"Oh dear," said Mrs Brown. "I don't like the sound of that!"

As soon as the others had gone, Paddington set to work. He washed all the breakfast cups and saucers and plates, and put them in a rack to dry.

Then he did the dusting, and after that he washed the dusters and the towels, and hung them up to dry.

When he had finished hanging up the dusters
and towels, he started making a special
chocolate cake as a surprise for Mrs Brown
and Mrs Bird when they got back.

Paddington liked cooking, and he was
soon busy mixing flour and cocoa and sugar
and milk together in a large bowl.

It wasn't until he put his paw in the mixture
to make sure it tasted as it should that he
saw he had made a mess with the flour and
cocoa. Worse still, the floor felt crunchy
under his feet where he had spilt some sugar,
so he got the vacuum cleaner out.

That was when his troubles started.

In his haste to tidy the kitchen he put the hose on the wrong end of the cleaner by mistake, and instead of sucking, it blew.

Paddington staggered back as all the old dust came out and rose into the air like a big, black cloud.

It landed everywhere: on the clean cups and saucers and plates, over the dusters and towels he had hung up to dry, over the table and chairs and floor. It even landed on his cake mix.

Paddington decided it was a good thing he was making a chocolate cake. At least it wouldn't show the dirt.

Paddington started work all over again.

He washed the breakfast things. Then he washed the dusters and the towels, and hung them up to dry.

And because the dusters were now wet, he thought he would use the vacuum cleaner to get rid of the dust.

This time he made sure the tube was on the right end.

Using the vacuum cleaner was much more fun and Paddington spent some time trying to write his name in the dust on top of the table.

It wasn't until he got as far as the letter 'd' that he noticed the mixing bowl was now empty.

He stared at the end of the hose wondering what to do next.

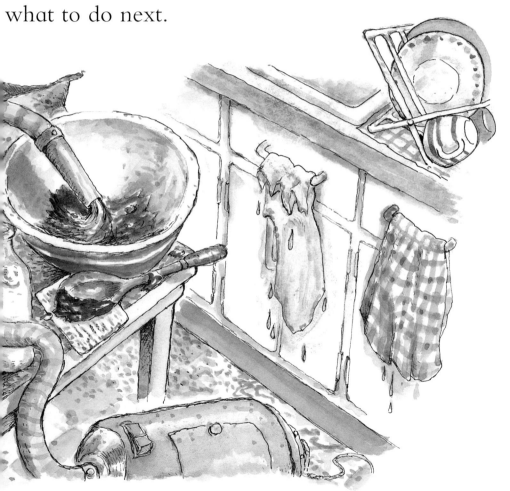

Paddington wasn't the sort of bear to be beaten, and looking at the end of the hose-pipe gave him an idea.

What had happened once could happen again.

He put the hose back on to the wrong end of the cleaner and then stood back, waiting to see if the cake mix would get blown out.

For a second or two nothing came out, and he was about to poke a spoon down inside to see if that would help, when there was a loud rushing noise.

One moment the kitchen was as clean and shiny as a new pin...

... the next moment it looked as if it had been raining chocolate.

Paddington gazed unhappily around the room. It was in a worse state than before. In fact, he couldn't remember ever having seen such a mess.

He gave a
deep sigh and
for the
third time
that day set
to work.

He washed
the breakfast
things. Then he
washed the dusters and
the towels, and hung them up to dry.
Then he scrubbed the floor and
washed the walls and polished the table and
chairs until it all looked as good as new.

In fact, he cleaned everything except
himself. But by then it was too late, for
there was a ring at the front doorbell.

"Paddington!" cried Mrs Brown. "Whatever
have you been up to? Are you all right?
You're covered in spots."

"*Brown* ones," said Mrs Bird.

Paddington looked at himself in the hall mirror and saw for the first time what a mess he was in.

"I think I must have a bad attack of 'Spring Cleaning Fever', Mrs Bird," he said.

Mrs Bird hurried into the kitchen, but she had to admit she had never seen it looking quite so clean. And if she wondered why Paddington had spots on his duffle coat as well as on his whiskers she didn't say anything.

"I think," she said, "you had better go upstairs and have a nice, hot bath."

Paddington thought that was a very good idea. He felt tired after all his hard work.

Afterwards, when he was safely tucked up in bed, Mrs Brown brought him his supper on a tray.

"You're looking better already," she said. "The rest must be doing you good."

"It isn't so much 'Spring Cleaning' that brings you out in spots, Mrs Brown," said Paddington. "It's all the clearing up you have to do afterwards."

First published in hardback in Great Britain by HarperCollins*Publishers* in 1986
First published in paperback by Collins Picture Books in 2001
Published as part of a gift set by HarperCollins Children's Books in 2007

5 7 9 10 8 6 4

Collins Picture Books is an imprint of the Children's Division, part of HarperCollins Publishers Ltd.
HarperCollins Children's Books is a division of HarperCollins Publishers Ltd.

Visit our website at: www.harpercollins.co.uk

Printed and bound in China